FOUL

PAUL HOBLIN

NIGHT FALL

FOUL

PAUL HOBLIN

darbycreek

MINNEAPOLIS

Darby Creek
A division of Lerner Publishing Group, Inc.
241 First Avenue North
Minneapolis, MN 55401 USA

For reading levels and more information, look up this title at www.lernerbooks.com.

Cover photograph © Joe Felzman/Taxi/Getty Images.

Main body text set in Memento Regular 12/16.

Library of Congress Cataloging-in-Publication Data
Hoblin, Paul.
Foul / by Paul Hoblin.
    p.   cm. — (Night fall)
ISBN 978-0-7613-7746-7 (lib. bdg. : alk. paper)
ISBN 978-0-7613-7949-2 (eb pdf)
[1. Horror stories. 2. Basketball—Fiction.] I. Title.
PZ7.H653Fo 2011
[Fic]—dc22   2011000931

Manufactured in the United States of America
3-44732-12226-9/15/2017

For MKTK.

Deep into that darkness peering, long I stood there wondering, fearing,
Doubting, dreaming dreams no mortal ever dared to dream before

—*Edgar Allan Poe,* The Raven

I may only be a sixteen-year-old kid, but on the basketball court, I'm a man.

I'm *the* man.

Almost seven feet tall and over two hundred fifty pounds of muscle, I might as well be *Superman.*

Ask anyone. Ask my best friend, Nate. Better yet, ask his dad, Sheriff Brady. He'll tell you in official police language that Ryan Johnson (that's me) is bigger, faster, and stronger than any other Bridgewater citizen. Case dismissed.

You can ask my adoptive parents, too. My

biological parents died in a car crash when I was a kid. I can hardly remember them at all. But ask my adoptive parents, and they'll probably even try to take credit for my genes.

Ask the Bridgewater High fans. They've been shouting my name for almost four quarters now. *Way to go, Rhino! You're the* man, *Rhino!* That's what everyone calls me—Rhino. Like when they want an autograph: "Rhino, will you sign this ball for me?" Or when they see me in the open court, getting ready to dunk. "Rhino! Rhino! Rhino!"

Ask any of these people and they'll tell you. I own this court. Every inch of it.

Put me at the ten-second line and I'll win every tip-off. Put me behind the three-point arc and I'll drain some threes. Put me in the lane and, well, if you're my opponent, you don't want me in the lane. On one end I'll swat your shot into the thirtieth row of the bleachers. On the other end I'll shoot my sweet hook or my floater. And that's if you're lucky. That's if I'm feeling nice. Otherwise I'll shoulder you to the floor and dunk the ball in your face. Or onto your face, if you haven't gotten up yet.

Just don't put me at the free-throw line. Please, please don't put me there.

That's the one place on this court where everyone's cheers turn to groans. It's the one place where I'm *not* the man.

If I'm Superman, shooting free throws is my kryptonite.

My muscular legs and arms go weak just thinking about it.

That's where I am now. The foul line. I already missed my first free throw, and the ref passes me the ball to attempt my second. I look around the stadium. Patty and Dale—that's what I call my adoptive parents—are in the middle of the bleachers. As always, they're biting their knuckles. So is Cindy Williams. She's a cheerleader and, according to me, the prettiest girl in school. Nate's dad, Sheriff Brady, probably isn't even watching. He probably has his eyes closed behind those shades he wears. He's seen his share of murders and mayhem, but those things are nowhere near as scary as my shooting form at the line.

And then there's the basketball recruiter. At least, I think that's what he is. He's been standing all game by the exit sign, watching us play. Watching *me* play. I'm used to it by now, of course. I may only be sixteen, but lots of recruiters have come to see my basketball skills. This is the first one to make me nervous, though. That's because he's wearing a Northern California State blue-and-gold sweatshirt, which is where my dad, my *real* dad, played ball. And it's where I want to play, too.

I return my focus to the basketball court. I watch Nate put his elbow into the guy next to him, ready to go for the rebound before I even shoot. I don't blame him. Everyone here knows I'm going to miss—even me.

I lift the ball over my head, let it go, and prove every one of us is right.

The ball clangs off the rim, and the other team grabs the rebound.

As usual, I'm the last one out of the locker room. Nate talked with me for a while, but then he pounded my fist and left. He knows I like to be alone after a game. Not that that's easy to do. Fans have started to wait around longer and longer. They want to clap me on the back or get my signature. Which means the only way I can be alone is to stay in this locker room until they finally give up.

And that's fine by me. It smells like stale body odor in here, but it's peaceful. Plus, I have a whole post-game routine. I sit in front of my locker and replay all of my highlights in my head—my rebounds, my dunks. As I do this I eat the granola bar Patty packs in my sports bag before every game.

My phone buzzes. I take it out of my pocket and look at the number. I don't recognize it, but that's not new. I get lots of calls from people I don't know. Recruiters get my number by contacting my coach or my parents. Fans get it however they can. Nate was once given a hundred bucks for my digits. He pocketed the cash and walked away without saying a thing.

Maybe it's the Northern California State guy calling. If it is, I don't mind the interruption.

"Hello?" I say.

"This is Ryan Johnson, right?" It's a male voice, but I don't think I recognize it. "Ryan *Danielson* Johnson?"

I'm not sure why he's saying my middle name like that, like it's really important or something.

"Call me Rhino," I say. If it is the Northern California State recruiter, I want to sound casual.

"I saw you play tonight."

"And what did you think?" I ask. "Am I college material?"

"I think you need to make your free throws."

Talk about a tough critic. "I scored thirty-eight points," I say.

"If you'd made your shots at the line, you would have scored ten more."

I try to stay calm. This guy is annoying, but I don't want to piss off the man who's going to get me into my dad's school. I look at my feet and take a deep breath. "I hear you," I say. "I'll work on it."

"You better," he says.

"I know, I know. Free throws win or lose games, right?" I've been hearing this from coaches for years, and I'm sick of it. We won today by twenty-four points.

I'm still looking at my feet, at my soggy shower sandals. I press my soles down. The sandals squish.

"That's one reason to make your foul shots, yeah."

"What's the other one?" I ask.

There's a pause.

"If you don't start making your free throws," the man says, "people are going to get hurt."

At first I don't know what to say. "What are you . . . who is this?"

But no one answers. Whoever it is, he must have hung up.

I sit there, staring at my phone. My heart is thudding against my ribs, and I tell myself to calm down. After all, I've received threats before. Lots of them. It's just part of being a basketball star. Earlier in the season the *Bridgewater Gazette* did a feature on me. The headline was "Rhino Bowls Over the

Competition." Someone sent me a copy of the article, but they crossed out the *o* in "Bowls" and replaced it with an *a*: "Rhino *Bawls* Over the Competition." The article included a black-and-white picture of me, and the person who sent it had drawn teardrops on my face. "This is what you're going to look like next game!" the person wrote.

Opposing fans tell me all the time that I'm going to get pummeled, crushed, even killed. It's usually pretty clear, though, that they're talking about the upcoming game. They mean I'm going to get pummeled, crushed, or killed *on the basketball court.*

But this threat feels more, well, threatening. Maybe I'll tell Sheriff Brady. Then again, I showed him the marked-up article as soon as I got it, and he couldn't do a thing about it. He said he totally understood my concern, but there was no way to track down the person who sent the article. "Unfortunately," he said, "you're going to have to get used to this kind of thing."

Like I said, it's all part of being a star.

I put my phone back in my pocket. All of a sudden I don't want to be alone anymore. I pull my sports bag over my shoulder and head for the door. My sandals squish with every step.

When I enter the hallway, I hear someone talking loudly. A girl's voice this time. It's Cindy Williams. She's leaning against the wall. Unlike most of the other cheerleaders, she hasn't bleached her hair blonde or made it completely straight, and I'm glad she hasn't. She has a winter jacket on, but she's still wearing her cheerleader outfit. The fabric of her skirt is pressed against the wall, and I can see even more of her legs than usual. She's talking on her phone. Loudly.

"So are you coming or not?" she says. After a little while she says, "Fine!" and hangs up.

She's upset. Her face looks hard with anger. She lifts her long dark hair with the back of her hand so her neck can breathe.

I swallow hard, try to get up the courage to ask if she needs a ride. I might be the man on the court, but I feel like a scared little boy when talking to girls. Especially Cindy.

She turns her head and sees me. I swallow one more time. I'm just about to open my mouth when she says, "Hey, Rhino. Mind driving me home?"

"I usually don't yell like that, I swear," Cindy says. We're walking down the hallway together. "That phone call just didn't go as I was expecting it to."

I know what you mean, I think. But I don't say anything. I just swallow some more.

"Thanks for doing this, Rhino," she says.

I nod, swallow.

"Sometimes my boyfriend can be a real creep." She's referring to a college dude she's been dating since forever. How can I compete

12

with that? "I mean," she says, "my ex-boyfriend."

Nice. Maybe I don't *have* to compete with it.

"He said he wanted to remain friends. His words, not mine. And for some reason I agreed. I don't know why I'm surprised he didn't show up tonight. I actually thought he'd be less of a jerk as a friend than a boyfriend."

We're at the doors to the parking lot now. It's the end of February, and the lot is iced over. I look at my car, squatting alone way in the back. I look at Cindy's bare legs.

I'm about to ask if she's going to be all right walking that far in the freezing air. But she once again beats me to it: "Sure you want to walk all that way in those wet sandals?" she asks.

I want to tell her it's no big deal, that I'm more concerned about her. But right now that seems like too many words for my mouth to manage. So instead I just nod again and push the door open. The cold breeze is stiff. We walk carefully across the patches of ice. When we get to my car, I unlock her door first.

"Thanks," Cindy says.

Before I can make it to my side of the car, Cindy reaches across the seat and unlocks my door for me. I get in, put the key in the ignition, and think, *Start. Please, please start.* Someday I'll drive a sports car, but right now all I have is an old, rusty, two-door piece of crap that I barely even fit in. My head brushes the ceiling unless I slouch.

Thankfully, the car *does* start.

"It's not too far," Cindy says.

She's telling the truth. In less than a mile she points to her house. My headlights swing across the house, and I see that it's big and white. All the lights are off inside. I pull into the driveway.

"Thanks again, Rhino," she says, opening her door.

I nod once more.

She pokes her head back in the car. "You're not a jerk, are you?" she says.

Finally, I speak. "I don't think so."

"I don't think so either," she says. She shuts the door and speed-walks toward her house. Her legs jitter in the cold as she digs for her keys in her jacket pocket. I wait for some of the lights to turn on, and I put the car in reverse.

When I enter my own house, Dale is sitting at the kitchen table, holding the landline phone. He's wearing one of his many turtlenecks, and I think about telling him for about the hundredth time that they look really lame. Maybe there was a time when guys wore turtlenecks, but that time is long gone. I swear, he'd wear turtleneck T-shirts all summer if they made them. He has some theory about his neck looking too long without them.

I shut the door behind me, and he turns his head. "Hi, Rhino," he says.

"Hey, Dale."

"Just got off the phone with a recruiter from Northern California State," Dale says. "He was at your game."

All of a sudden my heart is thudding in my chest again. "What did he say?"

"He says you need to work on your free throws."

T'wo days later, we're playing our archrivals,
St. Philomena's. It's late in the game, and
where do I find myself?

The free-throw line.

This time the game is close. We're down by
just one point when the ref hands me the ball
for my first shot. There's only a few seconds
left. I look around and see all the usual people:
Dale and Patty are sitting at half court. Cindy's
in a crouch, ready to spring into the air with her
pom-poms if I make the shot. Sheriff Brady's

stationed in front of the exit like always. The Northern California State recruiter is standing right next to him, wearing the same sweatshirt as last time. It's blue, with yellow letters across the chest that say NCSU.

I bring the ball above my head and let it fly. *CLANG!*

I can almost hear the collective sigh of everyone in the building.

I glance at the recruiter again. He's been standing there, next to Sheriff Brady, most of the game, and I wonder why. It turns out he didn't say anything about my free-throw shooting when he called my house—that was just Dale's way of joking around. "Still," Dale said, "you do need to start making those shots." Which is just like him. Ever since I became a star he's been giving me lots of advice. He never even played middle-school basketball, but I swear he talks to me sometimes like he's an expert.

I bend my knees and shoot.

Another miss.

Luckily, Nate's able to get the rebound and tip it off the backboard and into the hoop.

The fans go crazy. They mob the court. I have to sift through all the bodies, but finally I make it to Nate and say, "You saved me, buddy."

The two of us stand there grinning at each other. Over his shoulder, I can't help but notice the recruiter leaving. The overhead lights gleam off his pale, bald head. He breaks away from the crowd and slips out the door.

As happy as I am for Nate and my team, I wish the recruiter hadn't seen me miss those shots.

I'm on the court longer than the rest of my teammates. We're three games away from winning the conference championship, and after the game everyone wants a piece of me. Fans clap my back and punch my shoulder. An interviewer for the *Bridgewater Gazette* pulls me aside and asks me questions.

By the time I get to the locker room, everyone's gone. After taking a shower I sit in my usual spot, in front of my locker, dripping. I'm wearing my shower sandals again and eating my granola bar. I'm going through the game in my head when a locker door slams shut. I jump. I thought I was alone. When I check out the next row of lockers, I find Nate sitting there.

He's still in his basketball uniform. His school clothes and his winter jacket are in a pile next to him. When he sees me he picks the pile up and makes for the door. Nate's above-average in height, but he's really skinny. I can hardly see his upper body behind the bundle he's carrying.

"Everything OK?" I say.

"Sure," Nate says. He's trying to open the door.

"Here, let me help," I say. I'm in the middle of the locker room, and I take a few steps in his direction.

"I can open a door without the great Rhino's help," he says.

What's *his* problem? "I wasn't saying you couldn't," I tell him.

He takes a deep breath. The pile rises, falls. "Look," he says, "sometimes I get sick of being overlooked, okay? Why did you get interviewed?

I'm the one who made the game-winning shot."

I don't have time to respond. Even carrying the bundle of clothes, he's out the door and pulling it shut in less than a second. He dropped a sock, but I doubt he wants me to chase him down right now.

As I head for my locker I feel bad. Nate's right. He *should* have been the one interviewed. I scored another thirty points today, but he's the one who saved the game.

I'm imagining both of us getting interviewed together as I open my locker and something falls out onto the floor. I look to see what it is, and my body clenches.

It's a human finger.

Part of the finger is wrapped in a sheet of paper, but I can see the fingernail and the wrinkled skin below it. It's a woman's finger. The nail is long and smooth. It's painted half blue, half gold—Northern California State colors. I feel like vomiting, but instead I force myself to bend down and pick up the finger by its paper cover. The finger slides out and bounces on the hard floor.

I look at the paper I'm holding. It's a handwritten note:

Free-Throw Shooting Tip: Always hold the ball on your fingertips, not in your palm.

Just then I hear the door open. "Hello?" I say. My voice sounds desperate, and I tell myself to calm down. But then again, a finger just fell out of my locker, so why should I?

The door closes.

Maybe it was just Nate. Maybe he came back for his sock and left.

Whoever it was, I'm getting out of here. I toss my bag over my shoulder and take two long strides across the locker room. Out of the corner of my eye I see the finger. You can't just leave a human body part lying on the ground, can you? I turn and scoop the finger up in one motion and keep moving for the door. The sock's still there. Whoever it was who just opened and closed the door, he wasn't coming to retrieve missing clothing.

I scoop the sock up, too.

When I step into the hallway, I find Cindy once again leaning against the wall.

This time she's looking right at me.

I quickly drop the finger into the sock and hope she didn't see what I was holding. All of a sudden what I'm afraid of isn't the psycho who sent me the finger. It's grossing Cindy out.

"Don't you ever *wear* those things?" she says.

"What?"

"Your socks." She nods at what I'm holding. "Last time you walked out in your sandals, too."

I try to think of an excuse for carrying a sock rather than wearing it. But all I can come up with is, "Guess I just forgot." Then I add,

"Anyway, this one's all sweaty. I should probably put it in my bag with the rest of my dirty clothes."

I unzip the bag and put the finger-sock inside. When I look up, Cindy's staring at me. She doesn't know what to say. How do you respond to someone forgetting to put on socks?

"Hey," I say, filling the silence. "Did you see anyone leave the locker room right before I did?"

She shakes her head. "Sorry. Just got here," she says. "In the nick of time, it turns out. Any chance you could give me another ride?"

Like last time, Cindy's still wearing her cheerleading outfit. The first thing she does when she gets in the car is turn on the heat. She angles all the fans toward her legs. My eyes can't help following the air's lead. The fact that she's sitting makes her skirt particularly short.

"Eyes on the road, pal," Cindy says.

I lift my eyes up quickly. "Sorry," I say. "I didn't . . . I wasn't . . . I'm not . . ." I'm too embarrassed to finish a sentence.

Cindy's mouth breaks into a smile, though, so she must not be too upset. "Just trying to prevent an accident," she says.

I keep my eyes glued to the road.

"It's weird," Cindy says. "On the court you seem so tough. You're always glaring at the other team. You're *Rhino*. But off the court you're way different—just Ryan, I guess. Can I call you that? Ryan?"

I nod, which surprises me. I like the name Rhino. Plain old regular Ryan has always seemed boring—until now. Out of her mouth, I like how it sounds. It's like she sees me in a way no one else does.

I want to let her know I see her differently, too. "I was watching you cheer once," I say, "and I noticed you weren't actually *cheering* at all. I mean, you were going through all the motions, but your mouth was closed."

"Whoops," she says. "Guess I'm busted. I didn't know anyone had noticed." She's holding her wrists up and together, like she's ready to get handcuffed for breaking the laws of cheerleading.

"Your secret is safe with me," I say. "But why weren't you cheering?"

"I never really do. Even when I'm moving my lips I'm just lip-syncing. Cheering in unison seems kind of corny to me."

"Then why do you do it?"

"Because I love watching basketball."

Makes sense. "Why don't you play yourself?"

"I said I liked *watching* basketball, not playing it. I grew up going to Bridgewater basketball games with my parents, and as a cheerleader I always get front-row seats."

"Good thinking," I say.

Cindy puts her arm across her stomach and does a bow. "Why thank you, kind sir," she says.

I pull into her driveway. "We made it," I say, "accident-free."

"No thanks to you," she says, flashing her smile.

I look at her house. Once again there are no lights on. "Do your parents work at night?" I ask.

Cindy nods. "They work night *and* day. One's a pilot, the other's a global consultant. Don't ask me what that means, except that I'm home alone a lot."

"Is that freaky?" I ask. There's only one time I remember being left alone all night in my house, and that's the night my parents died in the car crash. I was five at the time. I remember waiting and waiting and finally getting out of bed. I wandered from room to room that night, and the apartment felt huge without my parents in it. These days I'm usually the biggest guy in any room I enter, but the idea of being alone in a house still makes me feel small.

"I'm used to it," Cindy says. "But if this is your way of asking to come inside, the answer is yes."

"Really?"

"You said you were a nice guy, right?"

I nod. She's pulling her door open, and I do the same.

As I climb out of the car, though, I catch a glimpse of my sports bag. Oh, yeah. There's a severed finger in there. Not to mention some crazy guy out there who did the severing.

"I *am* a nice guy," I say, "but I better go."

Cindy gives me another smile. "OK. See you later, Ryan."

As I drive home, I try to figure out what to do about the finger. I should report it, of course—I know that. But to who? I think about bringing it to Sheriff Brady. That seems like a good idea until I realize I saw him talking to the Northern California State recruiter. I know it's probably crazy, but what if the recruiter is the one who threatened me the other day? What if he put the finger in my locker? I *did* see him leave the court while everyone else was celebrating. And the fingernail is painted

Northern California State colors. Plus, whoever put it in my locker included a coaching tip.

OK, maybe I'm being paranoid.

The truth is, pretty much everyone seems like a suspect right now. It was a man's voice on the phone, so I'm going to assume whoever's behind all this is male. Beyond that, it could be anyone.

I take a left past County Hospital and an iced-over baseball diamond. Three blocks later I pass the town cemetery on my left, the car dealership on my right.

It might be a random stranger, but I don't think so. There's something about this guy. It's like he knows me. Knows my routines and when I'll be alone. He even knows what college I want to attend. I can't believe I'm considering it, but . . . what if it's someone close to me? Dale, for instance. I've been ignoring his basketball advice for years—could this be his way of making me listen? Or how about Nate? My best friend? I've never seen him as angry with me as he was tonight. What if those were his true feelings showing through? Worst of all, who does the finger belong to?

I turn right by the Bridgewater Library. I'm almost home now.

No, I tell myself. *It's not Dale. It's definitely not Nate. They'd never do such a thing. Right?* If it's not them, I'm back to the recruiter. And it is weird that a recruiter would spend an entire game talking to the local sheriff. Is Sheriff Brady in on it, too?

I ease into my driveway and park under the basketball hoop. Dale put it up the first day I started living with him and Patty. I look at our front porch. I helped build it last summer. I tell myself that I can trust these people. They've been taking care of me, after all, since I was five. They're practically my parents. And I have to tell someone about what's happening. A lunatic cut off someone's body part, and for all I know he has that person locked up somewhere.

I reach into the back seat for my sports bag and pick it up.

Of course, they're *not* my parents. Not my real ones. They're Patty and Dale. I've never called them Mom or Dad, and they've never asked me to.

I set the bag back down. I decide to keep the finger to myself until I'm sure I know what to do with it.

When I get inside, Patty and Dale are sitting at the kitchen table. They're looking right at me, as if they've been expecting me. "There you are," they say. "Where have you been?"

It's not like them to check up on me after a game. "What's going on?" I ask.

They look at each other. Dale nods at Patty as if to say, "Go ahead."

"It's your father," she says to me. "He escaped from prison."

"**W**hat are you talking about?" I say. "My parents are dead."

"No," Patty says. She's not looking at me anymore. She's looking at the table. "Your mother is dead, that's true—but your father . . . It's complicated, but . . ."

"Just let him read the article," Dale says.

He's holding a newspaper out for me to take. When I see the headline, the paper starts trembling in my hands.

Murderer on the Loose
According to authorities, Ryan
Danielson, convicted of killing his wife
eleven years ago, escaped early this
morning from Pineridge Heights, the
maximum-security prison where—

The paper drops from my hands and flutters to the ground. I stare at it and tell myself to pick it back up. But I can't. I can pick up a severed finger, but not this.

Dale says, "Look, Rhino—"

"You said they both died!" I scream. "In a car crash!"

Neither of them responds. Patty's still looking at the table, scratching at something with her fingernail. Dale pulls at his turtleneck like it's suddenly too tight.

"Well? What's going on?" I'm still yelling.

"We thought it would be easier this way," Patty says, still scratching the table.

"What way?" I ask. "Having both parents dead?"

"Isn't that better than having one parent in jail for murdering the other?" Dale says.

"That's not your decision to make," I say. "You don't get to decide what to tell me and what to leave out."

"Then whose is it?" Dale says. "If you were us, what would you have done?"

I don't know. I don't know because I can't think clearly right now. This information is too much.

"I'm sorry, Ryan," Patty says. She's still scratching away at the table. "I'm so, so sorry."

It's the first time I can remember her calling me that in years. Ryan. She was the one who originally invented the nickname Rhino, and she's been calling me that ever since. Until now. Now I'm Ryan Danielson *Jr.* Son of Ryan Danielson *Sr.*, the man who murdered my mother.

How did he do it? I wonder. *How* could *he do it? How could he kill his own wife?*

But then again, I don't want to know.

I ask Dale and Patty the only question I need an answer to: "When did he escape?"

"The article says he's been missing since last Tuesday."

My heart catches in my chest. Last Tuesday was when I got that call.

"Make your free throws or I'm going to start hurting people," the voice had said.

I'm used to everyone watching me closely, but this is different. Before, people were only interested in my moves on the basketball court—now they want to know about my life off the court. "Is it true?" everyone wants to know. "Is your dad a murderer?"

Reporters have their cameras and vans parked in front of my house. I feel like someone is following me at all times. I keep hearing doors slam without anyone entering the room. Floorboards creak even though, when I look, no one's walking on them. Last night I woke up to the sound of my bedroom window smashing shut, even though it's winter and there's no way I had it open.

The basketball court isn't much of a relief, either. I'm used to everyone screaming my name, but no one's doing that today. Everyone has gone quiet, as if they don't know what to say.

Not that they have much to cheer about. The man (my father?) told me he would hurt people if I didn't make my free throws, so I'm trying to make sure I don't have to shoot any. I do my best not to get open. That way, no one will pass me the ball. The few times the ball does end up in my hands, I quickly pass it.

My plan works really well until the end of the game. We're winning, and time is running out. The other team intentionally fouls me to stop the clock.

So here I am again, at the line. As always, Patty and Dale are sitting in the middle of the crowd. Cindy's in her crouch, though I doubt she or the other cheerleaders will jump into the air even if I make it. Sheriff Brady and the recruiter are once again standing next to each other. I watch Nate put his elbow in front of the guy next to him. Hopefully he won't have to get the rebound this time. Hopefully my shot will go in.

I release the ball and watch it float toward the basket. It rolls around and around the rim . . . but falls out.

If I had a choice, I wouldn't once again be here in the locker room alone. But I don't have a choice. I was surrounded after the game by news reporters. And even though we managed to win the game, these reporters had no interest in talking about sports. They just wanted to hear about my father.

I don't know anything, I kept saying. *Honestly. You know as much as I do.*

The locker room is the only place I can go to get away from all the questions. I'm sitting in my usual spot, afraid to open my locker, but equally afraid of leaving. There's probably tons more reporters waiting for me in the hallway. The only thing I can think to do is wait them out.

I wonder how long I'll have to be here. These reporters can't stay forever, can they? They have to eat sometime, right?

I unzip the side pocket of my sports bag and rummage through it for my granola bar. Instead, I grab something that's cold and slippery and round. I lift whatever I'm holding out of the bag.

My stomach lunges.

It's an eyeball.

Red veins shoot out of a brown iris like thin lightning bolts. There's a nerve dangling behind it.

Attached to the nerve is another handwritten note.

Free-Throw Shooting Tip: Never take your eye off the rim.

"What is *that?*"

I whip around. Nate's standing there, his mouth wide open.

"What are you doing here?" I ask.

He jerks his head toward the bathroom. "Taking a pee," he says. "Is that . . . man, what the . . . why do you . . ."

Nate's so freaked out he's stuttering. Oddly, I find this comforting. If I ever suspected him of being involved with any of this, I see now that I shouldn't have. His face is twitching in horror.

I decide right then and there to tell him everything. The threatening phone call, the finger, now *this*. I start to tell him about my dad but he interrupts me: "I already know all about that."

"Who doesn't?" I say. "It's been all over the news."

"No," Nate says, "that's not what I meant. I knew about your dad *before* he escaped."

I ask him what he's talking about.

"First put that thing away, man. It's creeping me out."

I'd actually managed to forget I was holding the eyeball. I put it in the same sock that's holding the severed finger and zip up my bag.

"Is that *my* sock?" Nate says.

I start to explain how I got it, but he brushes what I'm saying aside with his hand.

"I don't want to know," he says. "Just promise me you won't try to give it back, okay?"

I promise. "But how did you know about my dad before the article?"

Nate takes a deep breath.

"A couple weeks ago," he says, "my dad brought home a file—which isn't like him. He usually leaves his work in the office. From then on he spent every night sitting in the living room and reading that file. Whenever I asked him what it was, he just said it was research. I was able to get a few glances at it, though. It was a bunch of news clippings and court reports, and it all had to do with some murder a long time ago."

"My mom's," I say.

Nate nods. "Yeah. Except I didn't realize it at the time. The murderer had a different last name from you and lived in another part of the country."

"I was born in California. When Dale and Patty adopted me, they gave me their last name."

"I get that now," Nate says. He taps his pointer finger against his teeth, suddenly deep in thought. "What I don't get, though, is why my dad would be researching your dad *before* he escaped . . ."

I was wondering the same thing.

Nate shrugs. "Maybe that file has some answers," he says.

"It's still at your house?"

"I don't know," he says. "But I'll see what I can find."

As he leaves the locker room, Nate takes off his hooded sweatshirt and tosses it to me. The sweatshirt has his last name—Brady—stitched onto it, and he says maybe it will trick the reporters into thinking I'm him.

Once I put it on, though, it's pretty clear no one's going to be fooled for long. The sweatshirt is a little baggy on him, but it's skintight on me. The sleeves hardly make it past my elbows.

Still, I'll try anything.

I pull the hood over my head and peer out the door. To my surprise, the hallway is empty— or almost empty.

"I told them you'd already gone home," Cindy says. "Hope that's OK."

She's taken up her usual post across the hallway. She shrugs, palms up, pretending to actually be worried that she screwed up.

"You're a lifesaver," I say.

"Don't be too grateful," she says. "I only did it so you can give me a ride."

She's smiling her great, unique smile—top lip showing some of her gums, bottom lip covering just a little of her upper teeth.

"Fair enough," I say.

And I decide to tell her everything I just told Nate.

"Wow," Cindy says. She opens her mouth to say something else but can't find the words. I don't blame her—what's the right response after hearing what I just told her? "Wow," she says again.

We're parked in her driveway, next to her big, darkened house. Seriously, are her parents *ever* home? As I was talking, she took my hand from my knee and set it on her own. The car is turned off, and it's cold enough that most of my body parts have gone numb. But my hand's been tingling ever since she sandwiched it between her knee and palm.

What's cool is that I don't think *she* fully realizes what she's doing with my hand. She grabbed it like it was a totally natural thing to do. Now she's rubbing it the same way.

I tell her what Nate said about the file. "He's going to call me if he finds anything." It's only now that I notice she's shivering. Her teeth are chattering. "Looks like you need to get inside," I say.

She asks me if I want to come inside with her. "It would be a good place to hide out," she says.

But I tell her no. "I'm going to go home and try to get some sleep. Besides," I say, "all those reporters actually make my house the safest place I could possibly be. No one's going to try anything with all those cameras around."

As I'm walking up the steps of my front porch,
though, I realize I'm wrong. This place *isn't* safe.

In the corner of the porch I can just make
out the shadowy outline of a man.

He steps forward, into the light.

It's my father. My *real* father.

And he's holding a knife.

I should run, I think. *I should turn and run and scream until the reporters and the neighbors hear me.*

But I don't run, and I don't scream. Because I can't. I'm too afraid. Fear has paralyzed my legs and my vocal cords. All I can do is look.

Even if I hadn't looked at his picture in the paper, I'd recognize him. I haven't seen him in real life since I was five, but I've been picturing him in my head ever since. I remembered him being big—huge—and he is. All adults seem big when you're a kid, of course, but my father really is. For the first time since I was maybe twelve, I have to look *up* to see someone's face.

His eyes are wild, as if they're open too wide or don't blink often enough. When he finally does blink, the lids crash into each other. His hair is lopsided. His face is unshaven.

He strides toward me.

The chance to run is gone. He's too close now.

His knife gleams in the light.

Somehow my vocal cords start working again. "Why are you doing this?" I ask.

His looks at me, hard, as if he's trying to focus. His head shakes. His whole body spasms and shivers. He blinks again and lifts the knife.

"This . . . isn't . . . for . . . you," he says. He can hardly get out the words. It's like he's battling his own mouth.

He lowers the knife.

What does he mean? If the knife's not for me, who is it for?

I look more closely at the knife and realize I recognize it. It's big, maybe ten inches long and three or four inches wide, and it has a rust spot right in the middle of the blade. Patty has a knife that looks just like that. She uses it every time she carves meat or chops vegetables.

I realize I recognize my father's clothes, too. Or his sweater, anyway. His pants are orange and look like the ones convicts wear in movies. But his sweater—it's a *turtleneck* that's been torn to make room for his bulging throat.

"Where did you get that sweater?" I ask.

There's another pause.

"I . . . was . . . cold," my father says.

Before I know what I'm doing, I start to scream. "Dad! Dad! Dad!" But I'm not yelling at the father in front of me. I'm yelling for the father who lives in this house. I'm yelling for Dale.

All of a sudden more lights turn on. They're from all the reporters' vans camped out on the street. I turn and see the headlights beaming, and by the time I turn back to the porch, my father's gone.

Not that I care. I don't care about him, and I don't care about the headlights. I open my front door and run into my house. It's dark in here. I know every inch of this place by memory.

I race up the stairs three or four steps at a time, and I scream, "MOM! DAD!"

I'm in tears. *This knife isn't for you*, he said. And he was carrying my mother's knife and wearing my father's shirt.

"MOM! DAD!"

I burst through my parents' bedroom door and flip on the light.

They're both in there, lying on their bed, squinting through the bright light. They're blinking and rubbing their eyes.

They're both fine.

"What is it?" my mother says.

"Everything okay?" my father asks.

Their voices are groggy but concerned.

"Yeah," I say. "Everything's OK. Sorry. False alarm."

Their eyes are more open now that they've adjusted to the light.

"That's the first time you've called us Mom and Dad," my mother says. She's tearing up and smiling at the same time.

She's right. I think it's the first time I've thought of them that way.

We're standing there looking at each other,

waiting for our hearts to slow down, when my
phone starts vibrating in my pocket.

It's a text from Nate. *Found the file*, it says.

I wait until my parents' bedroom light goes out and they fall back asleep. Then I tiptoe downstairs as quietly as a guy my size can and sneak out the front door. The vans' headlights have been turned off. I keep mine off too as I drive away.

Nate's waiting for me on his front stoop when I pull up.

He puts his finger over his mouth as I walk toward him. "My dad's sleeping," he whispers. "Let's keep it that way."

He has a flashlight. I follow him to the back of the house to a closed door. "It's in here," Nate whispers.

The door is slightly ajar. We enter, but Nate keeps the door open. "This is an old door," he whispers. "Don't want my dad to hear it close."

The beam from the flashlight is pointing right at a big white box, and I realize we're in the laundry room. I wonder briefly if Sheriff Brady hid the file in the dryer. But then the beam swings around the room to the other corner, where there's a filing cabinet. Nate pulls open a drawer and fingers through it.

He pulls out a folder and whispers, "Here it is. My dad put it with his tax reports."

Together, the two of us go through the contents of the folder. We read newspaper articles and official reports. They all say the same thing: my father, Ryan Danielson, missed a free throw at the end of the national championship eleven years ago. Northern California State lost the game by a single point.

My father had a nervous breakdown. When the authorities found him, he was in his car in the parking lot of the stadium. His wife, my mother, was dead on the next seat.

There are pictures in the file of my mother, and they aren't pretty. She's covered in blood. Then I notice her face. That's when I have to look away.

"I'm sorry, man," Nate says. "We don't have to look at these anymore."

"No," I say, "it's not that. It's . . . she's missing an eye."

Nate looks closer. "She's missing a finger, too."

"Which means what? That my father has a thing for eyes and fingers?"

Nate nods, closes the folder. "Probably. According to my dad, serial killers do certain things the same way whenever they kill people. It's called their signature."

I think about all the times fans requested my dad's signature. I'm just a high school star, and I get these requests constantly. He played college ball. Then I think about the word *serial.* My dad's not just a killer, he's a *serial killer.* They say he went crazy after missing the free throw, but maybe he was already insane. Maybe my mom's body was just the first one they found. Maybe lots of people asked for his signature, and instead of using a marker, my father used a knife.

I think about the finger and eyeball in my sports bag. "All this time," I say to Nate, "I thought the worst-case scenario was that there was some woman out there who had been cut up and was either dead or alive. And that's so awful, obviously, but now . . . if my dad isn't stopped, there's proof he's going to keep doing this over and over."

I don't know if Nate's face has actually gone white or if it's the result of the flashlight shining on it. "I've been meaning to ask," he says. "Why didn't you tell someone sooner? I mean, the finger showed up days ago."

I shake my head. "I should have—you're right. It's just that I didn't know what was going on or who I could trust."

"You didn't think you could trust me?" Nate says. "Or my dad?"

"It was stupid. I know that. But your dad kept hanging out with that recruiter, and at the time I thought he was the most likely suspect, so—"

Nate interrupts me. "Wait. What recruiter are you talking about?"

"At the games," I say. "I kept seeing them talking with each other."

Nate taps his teeth, and I know he must be thinking hard. The teeth glare in the flashlight. "The guy wearing the Northern California State sweatshirt," he says.

"Yeah," I say, "and—"

But he interrupts me again. "That's not a recruiter," he says. "It's Bob Something-or-other. He's the new gravedigger."

I don't get it. "Why would your dad talk to him for two straight games?"

Nate shrugs. "He's always talking to people from the cemetery. He's a cop. Half his job is dealing with dead bodies."

"That's not the only reason," someone else says.

After all this time whispering back and forth, the new voice booms at us. Nate and I jerk our heads toward the laundry room entrance just as someone flicks on the light.

The rush of light is blinding, but after a second I can see well enough to recognize the man in the doorway. It's Sheriff Brady.

"You have no business reading that," he says. His voice is stern, but it's hard to be too intimidated because he's in his boxers. I think this is the first time I've ever seen him without his uniform. It's definitely the only time I've seen him without his sunglasses. He crosses the room and takes the file out of our hands.

Nate doesn't bother apologizing. "I'm the son of a police officer—what do you expect? What's the other reason?" he says.

"What?" Sheriff Brady asks.

"You said there was another reason you were talking to that Bob guy. The cemetery worker."

The sheriff looks up from the file and stares at his son. He has a beard that's starting to go white and that I'm pretty sure is designed to cover up some acne scarring. Nate has some acne troubles as well—maybe someday he'll grow a beard and become a cop too. I shift my gaze from Nate back to the sheriff and discover he's looking right at me.

"I'm not supposed to say any of this," he says, "but you deserve to know." He picks through the file until he finds what he's looking for. "The cemetery worker's name is Robert Elliot." He turns the open folder so it's in front of me and points to one of the sports articles.

Next to the article there's a picture of my father shooting the free throw he missed to lose the game. Someone—Sheriff Brady?—has used a highlighter to circle a guy in a suit standing well behind my dad. He's watching dad's shot with his hands on his hips. I recognize the guy. He has hair, but other than that he looks like the recruiter.

"Wait," I say. "He was—"

Sheriff Brady finishes my sentence: "Your father's basketball coach at Northern California State. *Coach* Elliot was also a gambler. And, I think, a murderer."

The sheriff keeps talking. He tells me all about Coach Elliot. Back when he was my father's coach he was famous for his competitive attitude and his temper. He was also suspected of betting on his teams, which is against the law. "We're talking huge sums of money," Sheriff Brady says. A year or so after my father missed that free throw, Coach Elliot was caught not only betting, but also threatening someone at knifepoint to lend him more money. He was sentenced to ten years in prison. "Just got out a couple weeks ago," the sheriff tells me. "And the first thing he does is move to Bridgewater. Seemed fishy to me. That's why I was talking to him at the game."

Nate's been listening too, of course, and he has the same question as me.

"Why do you think he's a murderer?"

Sheriff Brady tells us he's found evidence that Coach Elliot had bet big-time money on the outcome of the national championship eleven years ago. "When your father missed those shots, his coach didn't just lose the game—he lost a fortune. And he was furious about it.

"Besides," the sheriff continues, "serial killers don't just strike once. They do it over and over and always in the same way."

"Already explained that," Nate says. He really *should* be a cop.

"I tell you too much," his dad says. "At any rate, since I started looking into it, I've found evidence of other women killed in the same way as your mother."

"How do you know it wasn't my dad who did those things?" I ask.

"Several of the murders took place by casinos. That, plus Coach Elliot's history of gambling—"

"Well, then why wasn't he convicted in the first place?" Nate asks. He reaches for the file so he can take a closer look, but his father pulls it away.

"Because none of this evidence had been gathered yet," he says. "And because it looked like an obvious case of a mental breakdown." Sheriff Brady looks at me and sweeps his hand once through his beard. His voice goes soft, gentle. "Your father really did have a breakdown, Ryan. The only question is why— grief over missing those shots or finding his wife dead? When the authorities asked him questions, he could barely get a coherent sentence out."

"I know," I say. "I saw him tonight."

"In that case," the sheriff says. "I think it's your turn to talk."

I do. I tell him exactly what I've already told Nate and Cindy and about seeing my dad. When I'm finished, Sheriff Brady walks me to my car and asks for the sock in my bag. "I'll get this analyzed at the lab," he says. "Maybe it'll be enough to put this creep away for good."

It's only now that it fully hits me what I've just learned: my father's not a killer. He didn't murder my mom or anybody else. And I never would have learned this had it not been for Sheriff Brady. Until a few days ago, I didn't even know my father was alive. But by then my positive memory of him was dead.

In a way, Sheriff Brady just resurrected my father for me—the one I remember. The one who loved me and my mom. I want to hug the sheriff, but instead I just say, "Thank you, sir."

"Don't mention it," he says. "I know what it's like to lose a wife and the mother of your child."

He's starting to tear up, so he turns his face away and shakes his head. It's funny how you can live with someone most of your life and not put two and two together. I've known Nate since I first began living with my adoptive parents, and I've known all along that, like me, he doesn't have a mom. But I've never asked why. There's a story to tell, and maybe someday I'll ask to hear it. But not now. For one thing, I don't think Sheriff Brady is in the mood to talk about it. For another, I have another question about my father.

"But if my dad isn't here to scare me, why'd he break out of prison? Why did he come to see me? Why did he steal a knife?"

"One reason would be to protect you," the sheriff says.

"What's another one?" I ask.

He runs his hand through his beard again.

"Revenge," he says.

I feel as if I've dropped a huge amount of weight. Not literally, of course. I haven't shed any pounds lately. When I look in the mirror, I'm still huge. When Cindy puts her hand in mine, practically the whole thing—her fingers and all—fits into my palm.

Still, I feel lighter. And quicker. And happier.

Part of it has to do with the weather. A few days ago it suddenly got warm outside. It had been winter for months, and now it's spring. The ice has melted. There are puddles everywhere. No one has to wear jackets or boots or trudge through the snow.

Mostly, though, my sense of lightness has to do with what I told and learned at Nate's house.

Until then I'd been keeping what was going on to myself. And my secrets were heavy. The threats were weighing me down. So were the body parts in my sports bag. If whoever those body parts belonged to was still alive, she needed help. And the longer I waited to tell someone about them, the longer it would take to get her that help.

But now I've told Sheriff Brady everything I know. I've given him the body parts. And I feel lighter because of it.

Knowing that my father's not a killer makes me feel lighter, too.

We have an away game tonight in Rockville, and my whole team is lining up to get on the bus. We all see Sheriff Brady pull into the parking lot and stop behind the bus. He leaves his car idling and gets out.

Nate's standing in front of me in line and says, "Hey, Dad."

Sheriff Brady nods at him and then turns to

me. "Can I talk to you a second, Ryan?"

The words come out a little fast. He sounds excited about something.

The two of us walk away from the bus toward his car. When we're out of earshot, I ask, "What's going on?"

The sheriff hardly lets me finish my question: "I think we got the monster, Ryan."

"Really?" I say. "You got him? How?"

"His fingerprints were all over the stuff you gave me," he says. "Plus, the handwriting on the shooting tips matched his perfectly."

Now it's my turn to talk fast. "This is amazing. Where is he now? Is he in your jail cell? Is he in a cop car?" I tilt my head and look through Sheriff Brady's windshield to see if Coach Elliot is in the backseat. He's not.

The sheriff reaches up and puts his hand on my shoulder. "Not yet, Ryan," he says. "We're on our way to arrest him right now—just thought you'd want to know."

I take a few slow breaths to try to calm down. "Thanks, sir. For everything."

He claps my shoulder. "Looks like your team is waiting for you," he says.

I look behind me. The line is gone. Everybody but me is already on the bus. I try to pivot around to get on the bus myself, but Sheriff Brady squeezes my shoulder. "Almost forgot," he says. "We learned one more thing about the stuff you gave me."

"What?"

"It's old. Way older than a few weeks. He cut them off way before you missed any free throws. The only reason they were even preserved like that was because they were frozen. We still have to do more research, but my guess is he got them from the cemetery."

He's scratching his beard again—something he always seems to do when he's thinking. "Do you understand what I'm telling you, Ryan?"

"Yes, sir. You're saying my missed free throws had nothing to do with those body parts."

"Exactly," Sheriff Brady says. He claps my shoulder one more time. "Have a great game, Rhino."

I say thanks again and tell him that I'll do my best. But I'm just being humble. I already know Rockville doesn't stand a chance. This is the first time the sheriff has ever called me Rhino, but it makes sense that he did. For the first time in weeks, I feel like Rhino. I don't mind being called Ryan off the basketball court—in fact, I even like it. Especially when it's Cindy who's doing the talking. But on the court? Call me Rhino.

Better yet, chant it. At the top of your lungs. I can hear it now. *Rhino! Rhino! Rhino!*

Like I said, Rockville doesn't stand a chance.

By the fourth quarter we're winning by forty-two points. I've had my best game of the season: fifty-four points, twenty-eight rebounds, nine blocks.

I've also missed some free throws. Okay, a *lot* of them. Toward the end of the third quarter, Rockville started fouling me every time I touched the ball. It was the only way they could stop me from scoring. Even then it didn't always work. They would slap at my arms and yank my shirt as I muscled my way to the basket.

As the game continued the fouls got harder and harder. I think the other coach was mad at me for trying to embarrass his team, but that's not what I was doing. I was just enjoying being Rhino again.

I didn't mind the fouls. They were good basketball strategy. And I didn't mind missing the free throws, either. By now there was no way Rockville was coming back and, more importantly, my misses didn't mean someone else was getting hurt.

I spend the fourth quarter on the bench, watching our reserves finish the game. No, that's not true. I'm not actually watching the reserves play. Instead, I divide my time between thinking about Coach Elliot getting arrested and looking at Cindy.

She came to the game. Not as a cheerleader—they don't come to away games—but as a fan. The first time I spotted her, she was sitting with her friends, but unlike them she was watching the game really closely. She was also cheering really loudly. She may be a cheerleader who doesn't like cheering, but today she's making an exception. I'd just made a hook shot with two guys pulling at my arms, and when I turned to the crowd there she was, yelling my name along with all the other Bridgewater fans.

At some point, though, she must have decided to move, because now she's sitting next to my parents. All three of them are biting their knuckles, even though we're winning easily.

After the game I walk across the court and thank her for coming. She may not be in her cheerleading outfit, but she looks plenty great in jeans, too.

"You think I came to watch you, huh?" she says. "I told you I loved watching basketball, didn't I?"

"No," I say. "I mean, yeah. I mean, I just figured . . . you know . . . that . . ."

I'm stumbling around with my words before Cindy saves me. "You're right," she says. "I *did* come to see you play."

The way she says it, so straightforward, makes me study my hands in embarrassment.

"It was cool getting to talk to your parents," she says. "Or your adoptive parents . . . Patty and Dale . . . not your *real* ones . . . it's just—"

I bail her out. "It's OK. You can call them my parents. The two of them haven't missed a game since I was five, so they've earned the title."

"They volunteered to drive me home," Cindy says. "But I asked them to drop me off at the high school instead. I told them you always brought me home. Hope that's OK."

I tell her absolutely.

"In that case," she says, "I'll see you soon."

I don't think either of us could stop grinning even if we wanted to.

As I drive her home, I tell Cindy what Sheriff Brady told me. My dad's not the killer, I explain, Coach Elliot is. "He's probably in the local jail right now," I say.

Cindy hugs me so hard that I almost steer us right off the road. "Sorry," she says. But she doesn't unclasp herself from my shoulders.

I drive like that, with Cindy's arms wrapped around me, for a little while. Then she releases her grip and leans back into her seat. "Does this mean you'll finally accept my invite into my house?" she says.

"Definitely," I say.

A few minutes later we pull into her driveway. Unlike usual, the lights inside the house have been turned on.

I think Cindy's even more surprised than I am. She does an open-mouthed double take. "My parents," she says, "they must've come home early."

Her voice has gone quickly from shock to excitement. My car hasn't even come to a complete stop, but she's already unbuckling her seat belt and opening the door. All this time she's seemed so mature to me. So adult. She's a senior, so she's older than I am, and she dated a college guy. Plus she seemed so cool about staying in her house alone. When I asked her last time whether she got freaked out living in an empty house, she just shrugged her shoulders and said she was used to it.

But now she's acting totally different. She's acting like a kid. I babysit some of the neighbor kids sometimes, and Cindy looks like they do when *their* parents come home after dinner or a movie.

And honestly, as cool as she seemed when she was all mature, she seems even cooler now. As far as I'm concerned, you're supposed to miss your parents. I think again about being five and wandering my apartment while waiting for my parents to return. They never did, of course, not until my dad showed up the other night on my front porch. And I wonder whether it sometimes seems to Cindy like her parents aren't ever going to return, either.

She's out of the car already and just about to close the door when she stops. She sticks her head back in the car and says, "Sorry. I know I invited you inside, but . . ."

"No worries," I say. "Really. Go be with your family."

And like that we're both grinning again.

I'm almost home when I hear my cell phone vibrating in my sports bag. Keeping one hand on the wheel and my eyes on the road, I reach to the backseat, feel for the bag, and unzip it. I grab the phone and put it to my ear.

"Hello?" I say.

"You haven't paid attention to a word I've said, have you?"

It's a man's voice, low and raspy.

"Who is this?" I ask.

"You know who it is."

He's right. I do. It's Coach Elliot. His voice has been burned into my brain since his last call.

I'm surprised that I'm not more afraid. "Are you calling from your jail cell?" I say. I know from TV that the police let convicts make one phone call.

He ignores my question. "Twelve free throws," he says. "You missed twelve free throws today."

"How would you know?" I say.

He ignores this question, too. "You're just like your father," he says. "He never paid attention to coaching tips, either."

"That's why you killed my mother? To get my father's attention?" I think I'm screaming but I'm not sure. I turn into my driveway and tell myself to calm down. *They've got him*, I think. *The police have him.*

"That's right," he says. "No matter what I did, he wouldn't listen. Just like you."

"You're going to have to do better than digging up body parts from the cemetery to scare me," I say.

"Those body parts weren't from the cemetery," he says. "They were from your mother."

My senses go numb. I look at my other hand, gripping the steering wheel. I can't feel it, but I must be squeezing really hard because blood is draining out of it. It's getting paler and paler.

He's telling the truth. I don't need to ask Sheriff Brady to do any tests at the lab because I'm certain Coach Elliot isn't lying. I can just feel it.

What also seems obvious is that he's not in any jail cell right now.

"You're right, though," he continues. "My tips didn't work. You're just like your father. You need someone to take your girlfriend before you'll pay attention."

Cindy.

"But I just dropped her off with her parents," I say. I'm talking to myself, but I say it loud enough for Coach Elliot to hear. "Her parents weren't home," he says. "*I* was home."

I hear the sound of a girl crying.

Then nothing.

He hung up.

Before I know what I'm doing, I reverse out of my driveway and race back to Cindy's house.

When I get there all the lights are out again. I come to a screeching, crooked stop on her driveway and run toward her front door. It's slightly ajar. I shoulder through it and yell, "Cindy! Are you here?"

I run through the house, flicking lights on and screaming Cindy's name as I go. Downstairs there's a kitchen, a living room, a dining room. They're all empty, but there are signs of a struggle. Chairs are turned over. A wooden bowl of fake fruit has been knocked off the dining room table, the plastic fruit scattered across the floor. I scramble upstairs, still shouting, still flipping light switches. There's a long hallway and several bedrooms—but they're all empty too.

I race downstairs, not even feeling the steps and almost tumbling down them, and when I find the stairs to the basement, I make it to the bottom in no more than a few strides. "Cindy! Cindy! Can you hear me?"

But the basement is empty too. It's then that I realize I'm still holding my phone. I must have been carrying it all this time—in the car and now in Cindy's house—but I was too panicked to notice.

I look at my phone and realize that I have a message. I push the proper buttons and put the phone to my ear. It's the sheriff, telling me what I already know. They couldn't find Coach Elliot. He must have run away. Sheriff Brady says not to worry; they'll find him soon enough. "But in the meantime," he says, "be careful, Ryan."

He should have said, "Be careful, Cindy."

I stare at my phone some more. Then I look up the number of my last call and press *Talk*.

After one ring Coach Elliot answers. "I was hoping you'd call back."

"Just tell me what I need to do," I say. "Tell me what I need to do so you won't hurt her."

"Same thing as always," he says. "Make your free throws."

He doesn't say anything for a moment, and I think maybe he hung up.

"And keep the sheriff out of this," he says.

Now he really does hang up.

Our next game is in two days. I'm going to spend both of them shooting free throws in my driveway. In the morning I get up like usual and eat breakfast with my parents. Or I try to. I've hardly slept or eaten anything since Coach Elliot called.

"Not hungry?" Mom says. She's at the dishwasher and must have been looking right at me as I dumped an entire bowl of cereal into the trash. I shake my head no. "tired?" she says. "There are bags under your eyes."

"I'm just nervous about the game," I say.

I'm lying because I have no choice. Coach Elliot said I shouldn't tell the sheriff—but what he meant, I know, is that that no one should tip off the cops. The only way to guarantee that this doesn't happen is to keep Cindy's kidnapping to myself.

"You'll do great tomorrow night," Dad says. He's sitting at the kitchen table, talking over the newspaper. As usual, he's reading the sports section.

"You always do great," Mom adds.

"Says here you're the leading scorer and rebounder in the state."

Mom's on tiptoe, touching my shoulder. "That's why they call you the Rhino," she says. She gives me an encouraging smile.

"You called me it first," I say.

"My claim to fame," she says.

I put my hand on her shoulder and stare through tired eyes at my dad. What I told Cindy last night is true. They haven't missed a single one of my games since I was five.

"I better get going to school," I say.

They tell me to have a good day as I open

the front door. I get in my car and drive it three or four blocks before taking a left. I keep taking lefts until I'm back on my street. I wait and watch. When both Mom and Dad have left for work, I pull into the driveway again and take one of their places in the garage. I grab a basketball.

I stand in front of our hoop, fifteen feet away—the same distance as the foul line on a real court.

I think about my stats. Dad said I was the leading scorer and rebounder in the state. I wonder if the paper included a stat for free-throw shooting. Because I'm probably last in the state in that category.

That's why I'm out here. Practice. Tomorrow night my free throws are a matter of life and death.

I take a shot.

CLANG!

I need all the practice I can get.

This is the biggest game of the season. We're playing St. Philomena's again, and whichever team wins takes home the conference championship. The stadium is packed with both Bridgewater and St. Philomena's fans. Every time our student section tries to get a "Rhino!" chant going, the St. Philomena's student section responds with "Sucks!"

"Rhino!"

"Sucks!"

"Rhino!"

"Sucks!"

"RHINO!!!!"

"SUCKS!!!!"

Normally this is the kind of thing that would get my adrenaline going. I'd set out to prove my fans right and the other fans wrong. But today I can't concentrate. I can't narrow my focus until this game and this moment is all that matters to me.

Cindy is gone. Every time I look at the cheerleaders I'm reminded of this—not that I need a reminder. I wonder if anyone else even realizes she's missing. She's only been gone two days, so I doubt the school has bothered to call home yet, but by now the other cheerleaders must be wondering what's going on.

I tell myself to get my head in the game, but the truth is that I don't care. For the first time in my life, the outcome of a basketball game doesn't matter to me.

Except, of course, maybe I *need* to care. Maybe Coach Elliot is expecting us to win and he's going to take his anger out on Cindy if we don't. What I know for sure is that I have to make my free throws.

Just before the game I thought about pretending I was sick or hurt and unable to play. If I wasn't in the game, I couldn't get fouled. And if I couldn't get fouled, I couldn't miss any free throws. But even as I was thinking this I realized it wouldn't work. Coach Elliot would know I didn't play. I don't know how—I've looked all over the stadium and he's not here—but he would know.

And, anyway, that isn't the deal. He said I had to *make* my free throws—and to make them, I have to *take* them.

So far I've done both. I've taken six shots at the line, and I've made them all.

Maybe all my practice these last two days on my driveway is paying off. Or maybe I just got lucky.

Either way, every free throw I make energizes the crowd even more.

"Rhino!"

"Sucks!"

Like our last game against St. Philomena's, this one is close. We've been winning most of the game, but never by more than one or two baskets. As we enter the final minute of the game, we're up 67–65.

They have the ball, and they pass it around until there's less than ten seconds left. Then one of their guards swishes a three.

For the first time, St. Philomena's is winning. By one. With seven seconds left in the game.

Our coach calls time-out and draws up a play. Nate's going to try to throw a pass the length of the floor to me. I'll try to out-jump whoever's guarding me, catch the ball, and make the game-winning shot.

That's the idea, anyway.

Everything is going perfectly—Nate's pass is high enough that only I can reach it, which I do, but then, as I'm turning to shoot, practically their whole team wraps their arms around me. I'm in a straightjacket of human limbs, and I can't move.

Whistles blow from everywhere.

The final horn blares.

A foul is called.

Every player but me is sent to the bench. I walk to the free-throw line. The referee passes me the ball. The score is 67–68. If I make both free throws, we win.

I don't even want to think about what will happen if I miss.

The whole stadium has gone completely quiet.

I bend my legs, get my elbow out in front of me, and release the ball. It bounces off the front of the rim, off the backboard, off the back of the rim . . . and through the hoop.

There's a burst of cheering, but it goes away as soon as the ref passes me the ball again.

I stand there alone on the court, holding the ball with both hands, and I look for all the people who matter most to me. My parents are there, as always, biting their knuckles in the middle of the stands. Nate's sitting with the rest of my teammates on the bench. His dad is at the exit, watching me from behind his shades.

This stadium is packed—so packed that some fans have to sit in the aisles of the bleachers. It looks as if there isn't room for any more people.

And yet there are people missing, people who should be here but can't.

My birth mother, who was murdered. My birth father, who went crazy with grief when she was killed.

And, of course, Cindy.

I can't do anything about my parents—their absence is beyond my control—but I can bring Cindy back. If I can make this shot, I can save her.

I bring my eyes to the rim. I think about Coach Elliot's tips. *Never take your eyes off the rim*, he wrote. I don't. *Hold the ball in your fingers*, the other note said, and I do just that. I feel the texture of the ball, the dimpled leather, and—still looking at the rim—I lift the ball above my head.

If all this—all the threats Coach Elliot made and the people he's hurt—was about getting me to listen, it worked.

I let go of the basketball.

I'm still staring at the rim when the ball goes through it.

The crowd comes pouring out of the stands and onto the court. My teammates and the Bridgewater fans are all trying to get to me first.

I'm not paying attention to them, though.

I'm looking over their heads, behind my team's bench, at my sports bag. My phone's in there, and I need to get it.

People yell my name, smack my back, and tell me congratulations. They have their hands raised for me to high-five them.

But as far as I'm concerned, they're all in the way. I need my phone, and I push and elbow my way through this mob of people like I'm hacking through weeds and branches.

When I get to my bag, I take out my phone and dial Coach Elliot's number.

It's so loud on the court that I can barely hear the phone ring. When the rings have stopped, I say, "I did it. I made my free throws."

"I knew you would. Your father always said he didn't mean to miss, but I knew he just needed the right kind of encouragement."

I imagine my dad finding my mother.

"Where's Cindy?" I say.

"She can't come to the phone right now."

"Where is she?" I'm shouting into the phone, but no one seems to notice because they're all shouting, too.

"She's here, watching me dig her grave."

"You said if I made my free throws you wouldn't hurt her."

"And I won't. I'll make sure her death is as painless as possible."

I start to protest into the phone, but he has already hung up.

I sprint for the exit, sidestepping some fans and knocking over others. Sheriff Brady's standing next to the door as I run by. "Where are you going?" he shouts.

"The cemetery," I holler back.

There's no reason not to tell him now.

The cemetery is right in town—kitty-corner
from a car dealership and across the street
from a neighborhood coffee shop. Once
you enter the graveyard, though, you feel
completely isolated. You feel completely alone.

There are giant old trees lining the
perimeter of the cemetery, casting deep black
shadows into the already dark night. The road
I'm driving on is skinny, more like a path, and it
winds around in loops for no particular reason.

When I first entered I cut my headlights and

slowed down. I thought maybe I could sneak up on Coach Elliot. But it was too dark without my headlights, so I turned them back on.

Besides, maybe sneaking isn't my best strategy. I'm too big to be stealthy. Maybe I need to use my size to my advantage like I do on the basketball court. Maybe I need to push this psycho around like I just pushed my fans around.

Rather than being Ryan, maybe I need to be Rhino.

My tires squeal as I turn sharply on the cemetery road. If Cindy's still alive, I need to find her before she isn't.

A few seconds later I do. I'm just about to make another sharp turn when I see her in my headlights. She's alone and sitting on her knees. There's a pile of dirt behind her. Leaving the lights on, I slam the breaks and leap out of the car.

I yell her name and ask if she's all right, but she doesn't respond.

I wonder if I'm too late.

When I get closer, though, I see that there's a strip of fabric covering her mouth. I also see that she's been tied up. At the ankles and at the wrists. A horrifying image flashes through my mind of Cindy trying desperately to escape. But I don't see any cuts or wounds. She doesn't seem to be bleeding anywhere. Between her and the pile of dirt is a hole—a grave.

Cindy's making noises, frantic ones, and I think she might be gagging.

The strip of fabric is knotted behind her neck, and as I untie it I tell Cindy everything is going to be OK. But she continues shaking as her eyes get bigger and bigger. "It's OK, Cindy," I repeat. "I'm here."

"So am I," a voice says.

Before I can turn, I feel a *WHACK!* against the back of my head. I fall forward, hit the ground next to Cindy, and now I'm rolling, rolling—I get kicked in the ribs, but I can hardly feel it. I'm woozy. All the tension in my muscles is gone. I fall and land hard on something soft. My eyelids are heavy, but I force myself to open them.

It's dirt. I'm staring at dirt. I roll over and look up. I'm in the hole. Coach Elliot is standing over me. He's wearing his Northern California

State sweatshirt, and he's holding a shovel. His bald head is dripping with sweat.

The back of my head is throbbing. When I touch it, my hand comes back covered in blood. I'm having trouble keeping my eyes open.

I manage to say, "But I made my free throws. You said . . ."

I don't have the strength to complete the sentence.

My eyes are closed again, but I hear Coach Elliot say, "You were too late, Ryan. You were eleven years too late."

I open my eyes one more time and see dirt showering my body. My eyes close again and everything goes black.

I wake up, briefly, to a blood-curdling scream. The scream starts low—a man's—and gets higher as it continues. Whoever it is, he's in incredible pain.

I open my eyes and see a sneakered foot and the end of an orange pant leg.

"Dad?" I say.

But I feel myself slipping back into darkness.

When I wake up again, I'm surrounded by faces I know. My mom and dad are there, as are Nate and Sheriff Brady. Cindy's there, too. She's smiling at me.

My head is still throbbing. When I reach back to touch it, I feel a bandage.

Is it just me, or am I wobbling? That's when I realize I'm on a gurney.

"These flimsy things aren't made for a guy my size," I say, trying to sit up.

"The only thing that's made for a guy your

size is a basketball court," Nate says. He clasps my hand and helps me the rest of the way up. The gurney wobbles some more.

We're still at the cemetery; it's still night. Lights are flashing everywhere, from cop cars and from the ambulance behind me.

I have a ton of questions, but I start with the most general. "So . . . everyone's OK?"

"Everyone's alive and well," the sheriff says.

"Except the psycho coach dude," Nate says. He jerks his head over his shoulder.

"He's here?" I ask.

"Until someone bothers to move him," Nate says. "He's a goner."

"I want to see him," I say. I start getting off of the gurney.

"I'm not sure that's such a good idea, Ryan," my dad says.

"You need to rest," my mom adds.

But I'm already standing up and on my way to where Nate gestured. "Let him see," Sheriff Brady tells my parents. "He deserves it."

There's yellow tape surrounding the body, but I step over it. Coach Elliot's lying on the ground next to the grave he'd intended for

Cindy or me or both of us. His Northern California State sweatshirt is soaked in blood.

I step back and bump into the sheriff. "My father," I say.

Sheriff Brady finishes my thought: "He finally got his revenge."

"Did you arrest him?" I ask.

"He was gone before I got here."

"Are you going to chase him?"

"Eventually we'll have to," Sheriff Brady says. "But not yet. Cindy tells us he pulled you out of that grave. He's the reason both of you are alive right now."

I'm in my car with Cindy again. We're in her driveway. The lights are on.

"It's weird having my parents home all the time," Cindy says. Coach Elliot was killed almost three weeks ago, and her parents have been home every night since. I don't think they'll ever want to leave her alone again.

"Maybe I should walk you to the door, just in case," I say.

"Or you could finally come all the way inside," she says.

"I have been inside." I already told her about running through her house looking for her.

"Yeah, but this time I'll be there, too," she says.

We open our doors, but before we get out Cindy says, "I need to tell you something, Ryan."

"What?"

"I saw everything that night," she says.

"I know."

"No, I mean *everything*. I saw your father attack Coach Elliot—saw him use the knife. I was tied up, so I couldn't do anything. But even if I wasn't, I wouldn't have tried to stop him."

"He was saving your life," I say.

"I know, but I was glad your father finished him, Ryan. Not just glad to be saved but to see that monster pay. I felt so much relief." Her eyes are glazed over, distant, as if she's replaying that night in her head. She refocuses them on me. "Does that make me a terrible person?" she says.

I shake my head no. "I was glad too."

The two of us stare at each other for a while. When Cindy looks down, I follow her eyes.

We're holding hands.

"Shall we?" she says.

This time we make it all the way out of the car. As we enter her house, I think of how it looked that night, when I ran around flicking on lights and yelling Cindy's name. At the time I thought it was totally empty, but as I think back I'm not so sure.

I wonder if my dad was there. At the very least, he must have been close by.

I wonder if he's here right now, protecting me from any and all possible danger. I wonder if I'll ever see him again.

Everything's fine in Bridgewater. Really . . .

Or is it?

Look for all the titles from the
Night Fall collection.

THE CLUB

Bored after school, Josh and his friends decide to try out an old board game. The group chuckles at Black Magic's promises of good fortune. But when their luck starts skyrocketing—and horror strikes their enemies—the game stops being funny. How can Josh stop what he's unleashed? Answers lie in an old diary—but ending the game may be deadlier than any curse.

THE COMBINATION

Dante only thinks about football. Miranda's worried about applying to college. Neither one wants to worry about a locker combination too. But they'll have to learn their combos fast—if they want to survive. Dante discovers that an insane architect designed St. Philomena High, and he's made the school into a doomsday machine. If too many kids miss their combinations, no one gets out alive.

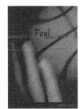

FOUL

Rhino is one of Bridgewater best basketball players—except when it comes to making free throws. It's not a big deal, until he begins receiving strange threats. If Rhino can't make his shots at the free throw line, someone will start hurting the people around him. Everyone's a suspect: a college recruiter, Rhino's jealous best friend, and the father Rhino never knew—who recently escaped from prison.

LAST DESSERTS

Ella loves to practice designs for the bakery she'll someday own. She's also one of the few people not to try the cookies and cakes made by a mysterious new baker. Soon the people who ate the baker's treats start acting oddly, and Ella wonders if the cookies are to blame. Can her baking skills help her save her best friend—and herself?

THE LATE BUS

Lamar takes the "late bus" home from school after practice each day. After the bus's beloved driver passes away, Lamar begins to see strange things—demonic figures, preparing to attack the bus. Soon he learns the demons are after Mr. Rumble, the freaky new bus driver. Can Lamar rescue his fellow passengers, or will Rumble's past come back to destroy them all?

LOCK-IN

The Fresh Start Lock-In was supposed to bring the students of Bridgewater closer together. Jackie didn't think it would work, but she didn't think she'd have to fight for her life, either. A group of outsider kids who like to play werewolf might not be playing anymore. Will Jackie and her brother escape Bridgewater High before morning? Or will a pack of crazed students take them down?

MESSAGES FROM BEYOND

Some guy named Ethan has been texting Cassie. He seems to know all about her—but she can't place him. Cassie thinks one of her friends is punking her. But she can't ignore how Ethan looks just like the guy in her nightmares. The search for Ethan draws her into a struggle for her life. Will Cassie be able to break free from her mysterious stalker?

THE PRANK

Pranks make Jordan nervous. But when a group of popular kids invite her along on a series of practical jokes, she doesn't turn them down. As the pranks begin to go horribly wrong, Jordan and her crush Charlie work to discover the cause of the accidents. Is the spirit of a prank victim who died twenty years earlier to blame? And can Jordan stop the final prank, or will the haunting continue?

THE PROTECTORS

Luke's life has never been "normal." His mother holds séances and his crazy stepfather works as Bridgewater's mortician. But living in a funeral home never bothered Luke—until his mom's accident. Then the bodies in the funeral home start delivering messages to him, and Luke is certain he's going nuts. When they start offering clues to his mother's death, he has no choice but to listen.

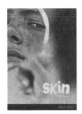

SKIN

It looks like a pizza exploded on Nick Barry's face. But a bad rash is the least of his problems. Something sinister is living underneath Nick's skin. Where did it come from? What does it want? With the help of a dead kid's diary, Nick slowly learns the answers. But there's still one question he must face: how do you destroy an evil that's inside you?

THAW

A storm caused a major power outage in Bridgewater. Now a project at the Institute for Cryogenic Experimentation is ruined, and the thawed-out bodies of twenty-seven federal inmates are missing. At first, Dani didn't think much of the news. Then her best friend Jake disappeared. To get him back, Dani must enter a dangerous alternate reality where a defrosted inmate is beginning to act like a god.

UNTHINKABLE

Omar Phillips is Bridgewater High's favorite local teen author. His Facebook fans can't wait for his next horror story. But lately Omar's imagination has turned against him. Horrifying visions of death and destruction come at him with wide-screen intensity. The only way to stop the visions is to write them down. Until they start coming true . . .

SOUTHSIDE HIGH

ARE YOU A SURVIVOR?

The Alliance

Bad Deal

Beaten

Benito Runs

Dance Team

Deadly Drive

THE FIGHT

Full Impact

Overexposed

Plan B

Recruited

Shattered Star

check out all the books in the

SURVIVING · SOUTH SIDE

collection

MIDNIGHT

TICK . . . TOCK . . . TICK . . . TOCK.
WILL YOU MAKE IT PAST MIDNIGHT?

CHECK OUT ALL OF THE TITLES IN THE MIDNIGHT SERIES